The Berenstain Bears®

and the Tooth Fairy

Jan & Mike Berenstain

The Tooth Fairy
has a job that's funny.
She takes away teeth
and puts back money!

HARPER FESTIVAL
An Imprint of HarperCollinsPublishers

The Berenstain Bears and the Tooth Fairy
Copyright © 2012 by Berenstain Publishing, Inc.
Printed in the U.S.A. All rights reserved. No part of this book may be used or reproduced in any manner whatsoever
without written permission except in the case of brief quotations embodied in critical articles and reviews.
For information address HarperCollins Children's Books, a division of HarperCollins Publishers, 10 East 53rd Street, New York, NY 10022.
www.harpercollinschildrens.com
Library of Congress catalog card number: 2011945726
ISBN 978-0-06-207549-9
12 13 14 15 16   CWM   10 9 8 7 6 5 4 3
❖
First Edition

Sister Bear wasn't a little cub anymore. After all, she was almost seven years old. She had three grown-up teeth already—two on the bottom and one on the top. When her baby teeth came out, Mama and Papa had her put them under her pillow.

"While you are sleeping, the Tooth Fairy will come," they explained.
"She will take your baby tooth and leave money in its place."

So Sister would put the baby tooth under her pillow. When she woke up in the morning, she found a shiny new quarter in its place.

Sister loved the Tooth Fairy. She thought the Tooth Fairy
was almost as good as Santa Claus and the Easter Bunny.

One day, Sister was playing with her best friend, Lizzy Bruin. "Guess what?" said Lizzy.

"What?" said Sister.

"I have a loose tooth," said Lizzy. She opened her mouth wide. "See? It wiggles!" She wiggled it back and forth.

"When it comes out," said Sister, "the Tooth Fairy will bring you a quarter."

"A quarter?" said Lizzy. "When my teeth come out, the Tooth Fairy brings me a whole dollar."

"A dollar?" said Sister, shocked. How come the Tooth Fairy only brought her a quarter? It wasn't fair!

Sister ran home to Mama and Papa. "Lizzy says that when her baby teeth come out, she gets a whole dollar!" she said. "Why does the Tooth Fairy only bring me a quarter?"

"Well," said Mama, "some parents add a little extra to the money the Tooth Fairy brings. But we think that's the Tooth Fairy's job."

"Besides," added Papa, "sometimes the price of things goes up, like gas. The price of gas for our car went up twenty cents just last week! Maybe the same thing happens with teeth."

"Do you think the price of my teeth will go up?" asked Sister.

"We'll just have to wait and see," said Mama.

After a few days, Sister forgot all about the Tooth Fairy. She was a busy cub and had things to do. She played house with Lizzy. She played baseball with Brother and Cousin Fred. She painted pictures of butterflies and flowers.

She went fishing with Papa and shopping with Mama.

Lizzy's birthday was coming up. Sister was looking forward to going to a big birthday party.

Then, one morning at breakfast, Sister was eating one of Mama's yummy muffins. She felt something different in her mouth. She pushed her tongue against one of her front teeth. It moved a little bit. She had another loose tooth!

"Mama! Papa!" she said. "My tooth is loose! Look, it wiggles!"

"That's nice, dear," said Mama. "When it comes out, put it under your pillow and the Tooth Fairy will bring you a quarter."

"Maybe this time I'll get a whole dollar!" said Sister.

"Oh, yes," said Papa. "The Tooth Fairy is paying more these days."

"That's right," said Mama. "You explained that the price of teeth is going up—like gas."

"Oh boy!" said Sister. "A whole dollar!" She thought about what she could get with that dollar. But the loose tooth had to come out first.

Sister began to wiggle her loose tooth whenever she could. She wiggled it with her tongue. She wiggled it with her fingers. Day after day, she wiggled it and wiggled it. It grew looser and looser. But it did not come out. It was annoying. It made it hard to chew and Sister was always fussing over it.

"I sure wish that tooth would come out," muttered Brother as Sister wiggled away. "All that wiggling is getting on my nerves."

"When it comes out," said Sister, "I might get a whole dollar!"

"I never got a whole dollar," grumped Brother.

"That was back when teeth were still cheap," explained Sister.

The day of Lizzy's birthday party soon came. Sister had her present all wrapped—a new Bearbie doll for Lizzy's collection. All the cubs began to arrive at Lizzy's house. Lizzy was having an old-fashioned birthday party with old-fashioned party games.

They played Pin the Tail on the Donkey; musical chairs; charades; Duck, Duck, Goose; hit the piñata; and bobbing for apples.

Bobbing for apples was hard. You had to hold your hands behind your back while you tried to bite an apple floating in a tub of water. The apples kept bobbing out of the way. But Sister was determined to get an apple. She lunged at one of the apples and bit down, hard! She felt something come loose in her mouth. Her loose tooth was out! It was stuck in the apple.

Proudly, Sister brought her baby tooth home wrapped in a tissue.

"Look, Mama! Look, Papa!" she said. "My tooth finally came out. Now I can put it under my pillow, and maybe the Tooth Fairy will bring me a whole dollar!"

As Sister got ready for bed that night, she grew thoughtful.

"Mama," she asked, "where does the Tooth Fairy get all that money?"

"I haven't a clue," said Mama. "Now brush your teeth—the ones that are left, anyway."

Carefully, Sister placed her tooth under her pillow. Mama and Papa kissed her good night, and she lay awake for a while thinking about finding a dollar in the morning. Then she drifted off to sleep.

During the night, Sister had a dream. She dreamed the Tooth Fairy came tiptoeing into her room. The Tooth Fairy was very beautiful. She wore a pink dress and had butterfly wings. She had a flower in her fur and a magic wand. She came over to Sister's bed and smiled down at her. Then, she reached under the pillow and . . .

Sister woke up!

It was morning and the sun was streaming through the window. The Tooth Fairy was not there.

Sister reached under her pillow with great excitement and felt something crisp and crinkly. It was a brand-new dollar bill.

"What a relief!" said Sister as Mama and Papa came in. "I was afraid the price of teeth might be coming down again."

"Your baby teeth are very precious," said Papa. "Every one that comes out shows that you are growing up fast. They're worth every penny!"

"You mean every dollar," said Sister, with a big missing-tooth grin.

Mama and Papa just looked at each other and grinned, too.